Cormac, King of the Leprechauns

Mike O'Donovan

© 2006

By the same author

"Timmy And The Dragon"

"The Amazing Tales of Mike O'Donovan"

"Short Tall Tales"

Published by:

Blarney Publications
44 Halldene Avenue
Bishopstown
Cork
Ireland

Tel: 00 353 21 4530422
00 353 86 2849843

Sketches by Eugene D'Arcy
Printed by City Print, Cork. Tel: 021 4545655

ISBN: 0-9543530-3-X

For Boys and Girls
of all ages

& in particular my Grandsons

Gareth & Ebhan

Cormac, King of the Leprechauns

Cormac sat on his high throne and sighed a weary sigh. All the excitement of his visit to the Otherworld to help his friend Timmy in his fight against the evil dragon had died down and Cormac was now finding the going tough. It was very boring for him to sit on a throne day after day listening to the cackling of all of the thousands of other leprechauns around him whose only interests appeared to be living the good life. They were all very funny and witty but could not see beyond today. All was calm except for a nagging feeling in the pit of his stomach that something was in the air which caused Cormac to have a deep sense of foreboding, his magic mind warning him of impeding disaster. Images of the evil Giles De Montefiore flashed before him, but he figured that Giles was a person from the past and was well gone.

Cormac had been elected king of the leprechauns because of his great wisdom and knowledge, but he had his hands full, for the rest of the leprechauns did exactly as they pleased not showing much respect for Cormac or his position, all they wanted was the high life. Cormac looked down on the happy throng as they sang and danced through the streets and admired them with some pride.

Cormac's wife Orla skipped past him leading a group of dancers doing the "Siege Of Ennis". The male leprechauns were all dressed in green suits with matching ribboned hats and shiny black buckled shoes. The lady leprechauns wore green apron type costumes with shawls covering their little shoulders. The groups of tiny dancers looked very attractive as they wended their way around

Cormacs high throne. Cormac caught Orla's eye and beckoned to her. Orla left the group and came to him. "Please get help from Sean and check the crocks of gold, then report back to me, we must maintain our guard. Orla was one of the few in the community Cormac could trust to maintain some semblance of sanity. Orla left and was followed by Sean, one of the leprechaun elders.

King Cormac waited and watched the all singing and all dancing little people while ruminating on life and Michael Flatley whose success at the dance had ruined the leprechauns completely, they all now imagining that they could do world tours and be good enough to appear on Broadway, "dreamers, dreamers, every one" thought Cormac as he watched his people battle it out with each other while introducing very complicated fancy footwork in their efforts to beat any rival. Cormac cursed Michael Flatley under his breath thinking, "That fella has a lot to answer for". Orla was soon to return with Sean. "Everything is intact, all the crocks of gold are filled to the brim as they should be, you worry too much Cormac, the Otherworlders do not have the wit or the power to ever find out where we are or where the gold is, so relax my husband, come join me in a dance". Cormac decided that Orla was probably right and hobbled down the steps from his throne to join his wife in a two-hand reel. He decided that maybe he should listen to Orla more often and that he should forget his responsibilities for a while. A crowd of cheering hand-clapping leprechauns gathered to surround the couple as they twirled around to the sound of vibrant Irish music, and the gaiety and the night rolled on into day.

Giles De Montefoire had discovered something of great importance during his visit to the valley when he had used

a fiery dragon to try to destroy the people and take their land only to be foiled by the magic of the leprechauns. That discovery was that there actually were leprechauns in the area, and everybody knew that where there were leprechauns there was gold. Giles was overcome with greed at the thought of getting his grubby hands on the fortunes of the little people and that thought caused droplets of saliva to roll down his chin and stick to his scraggy grotty beard.

The leprechauns had succeeded in destroying his castle and the dragon by using their magic, but Giles had successfully eluded capture and elimination by using his guile and his own magic. He had used all of his sorcery to simply disappear, then to re-appear in his dark stinking castle high up in the mountains but the effort of it all had drained him. Magic was very useful but was very weakening, even for a regular practitioner. Giles bided his time and plotted and planned, figuring out a way to get the gold. Giles was a very determined and evil man, also, he had a score to settle with the little people, so not alone was he to attempt to steal the leprechauns fortune and leave them penniless, he was also out to seek revenge and punish them for what he saw was their sin in preventing him from taking over the valley and using the local people as slaves in his castle and on his stolen lands.

The sound of much snoring seeped out through the grassy earth covering the fairy fort near Timmy's house and was the cause of severe annoyance to the worms who lived in that area causing them to mutter curses of complaint that they had to inhabit the same place as the leprechauns. Between the dancing, the singing, the music, and the

snoring, the worms were driven to distraction. The humans could not hear the leprechauns of course, they having different ear fittings to the worms, but that was of no consolation to the worms at all.

Giles De Montefiore awoke suddenly and sat at the side of his bed raising his two clenched fists in triumph. He had dreamed a dream and now knew how he could outwit the leprechauns. He had a plan. He called out loudly, "Minkin, Minkin, get yourself in here, NOW". A grey faced warted ugly old witch entered Giles chamber and was to witness the sight of him sitting on his bed wearing a shabby nightgown which in the distant past might have been white, but it was now a dirty grey colour and displayed the droppings of years of food. His filthy nightcap appeared to be glued to the long greasy hair which hung limply from his head. His open yawning mouth displayed rows of rotten teeth.

Minkin stood well back to avoid the terrible smells coming from his body, his clothes and his breathe. "What is it master?"

Minkins voice sounded like a mangled animal in distress. When she spoke the vibrations from her voice activated a long wart she carried on her nose causing it to quiver in time to her voice like a conductors baton, accompanying her as she spoke.

"I have the solution to my problem concerning the horrible little nothings who dress in green, I intend to give them the foul treatment, last used during the revolt of the peasants. If memory serves me, it serves me well, for as far as I can remember we beat the stuffing's out of the idiots who ducked and dived in their vain attempts to avoid us"

"The gods of war and evil are definitely on your side master, to have such inspiration, it is indeed a marvellous plan" Minkin clapped her hands in appreciation causing one of her fingers fall off and drop to the ground. Giles rubbed his hands over his stomach in satisfaction while smiling a crooked smile. "Now woman, get thee to the kitchen and prepare my cornflakes and remember, I like them nice and soggy and without fingers"

Giles laughed a horrible laugh which echoed and echoed until it reached the deepest bowls of his dark castle causing the rats to scatter and run seeking shelter from the sound of his voice. Minkin rushed from the bedchamber to do her masters bidding. Giles liked his cornflakes.

The worms living in the same fairy fort as the leprechauns were in a state of ugly rebellion because of their lack of sleep due to the leprechauns giddy lifestyle and partying, the worms changing from their usual placid and quiet ways into creatures of revolt. They eventually decided to call a meeting of all the worms in order to try to resolve the very serious problem. An assembly point was arranged outside the hillock so they could meet in peace without the noise of snoring, singing, and music. Seamus, the head worm stood tall on a rostrum and shouted out, "Brostaig ort, Hurry up, the meeting is about to start." The hill was suddenly alive with the sight of thousands of worms breaking through the grassy surface to wriggle towards the meeting place. They all looked very cross, tired, and weary from lack of sleep.

Cormac felt that danger was to be expected, but he was not sure yet what that danger was or what form it would

take. He decided to inform Orla of his fears and ask her opinion. Reaching under his throne he picked up a thick blackthorn stick he had hidden there many years before and called his wife to bring her into his confidence. "Cad é sin? What is that?" Asked Orla. "This is a very ancient stick" "Cé do é sin?" "Who is it for?"

"It was given to us leprechauns by the ancient gods to be used only in special circumstances and I can feel and sense that there are special circumstances on the way, when we both hold this magic stick it should bring someone from the spirit world and help us in the future".

Cormac and Orla made their way along the town and through the gates to the main hall in their little green castle where they then closed and bolted the large doors behind them before sitting across from each other at a very old table. Cormac placed the stick across the table and requested that Orla hold the other end. As soon as she placed her hands on the stick the hall was lit up by a series of brilliant flashing lights and a loud thunderous noise which shook the castle but was soon to cease leaving the lights to slowly unite and form a ghostly figure which floated above them. A croaking voice was heard to come from the wavering thing floating in the air.

"Fion, fion, please"

"Wine? It wants wine?, Queried Orla. "Whist Orla my love" said Cormac as he poured wine from a large jug on the table into a goblet and raised it up in the air. A hand materialised to grab the goblet and then all they could hear was the sound of glugging and gasping. "Ahh, that's me first drink in centuries and it was grand, eh, could I trouble ya for another? By the way, my name is Umbhar". Cormac was about to reach for jug again when Orla stopped him by grabbing his arm saying "I thought this spirit was called

here to help us, all he seems to want to do is drink, give him no more". Cormac had to stop himself in his natural hospitality but he knew that Orla was right, he also realizing again that he had made a wise choice all those hundreds of years ago in choosing the beautiful and intelligent Orla as his wife. What Cormac and orla did not realize that there was also trouble in the spirit world between the different factions who operated on political party lines much the same as humans, consequently the amount of name-calling and character assassination among the spirits was enormous.

Meanwhile, back outside the fairy fort things were getting a bit on the rowdy side at the mass protest meeting held by the worms. Some of the younger hotheads were for declaring all out war on the leprechauns, but after much shouting and roaring and banging of the chairman's gavel order was restored and older wiser heads prevailed. After some more debate it was proposed to send a delegation of worms to meet the leprechauns and a letter of protest signed by all the worms of the parish to be handed in. This motion was passed unanimously and the meeting broke up peacefully.

The problems in the spirit world were fairly commonplace except that we would not usually expect anything commonplace in that area would we? Anyway, there were some very clever ancient spirits out there in their own little world and some not so clever spirits. Some of the more clever spirits looked down on the more stupid spirits and that attitude created tremendous differences in that community, causing the minority clever spirits to use the majority stupid types to make right dopes out of them. There were some right eejit spirits who got all of the

crummy jobs to do, one of them, a dope the name of Umbhar was usually sent out on jobs nobody else wanted. It was well known that Umbhar was the biggest eejit of all. It was also well known the he was fond of the drink, was not very bright, and also leprechauns were not the most popular creatures in the spirit world because of their wild crazy ways, so the leprechauns were lumbered with a halfwit of a spirit to help them, but they were not to know that of course.

Giles and Minkin sat at a long table, he sipping wine while reading from a big book on black magic and sorcery, she busy mixing ingredients in a large cauldron which belched occasionally giving off the most putrid smelling steam. They were busy plotting the downfall of their enemies, the leprechauns. Giles turned to Minkin and roared loudly, "Airgead! Airgead! Money! Money! That's what life is all about, you wart faced old hag" Giles gleefully rubbed his hands together thinking about the fortune that was soon to be his and laughed so much that he fell to the ground from his chair. Minkin threw her eyes to heaven and continued with her task of stirring the pot. Giles continued to laugh while lying flat on his back scaring the fat cockroaches scurrying around him. Some days later the strange looking pair left their castle laden down with large bottles of a magic potion.

Umbhar slowly drifted down from his place above and sat at the table next to Orla and Cormac. He was tall with long grey hair above a wrinkled gullible looking face, was dressed in a long white robe and looked as pale as a corpse. "You have a problem?" The two rulers of the leprechaun kingdom went into some detail and told him told him of the

fears of Cormac and his strange feelings of disaster to come. Umbhar listened to their story nodding his head every now and again. At their conclusion he scratched his long white beard and spoke in very knowledgeable and knowing tone. "This reminds me of a very similar case I was on many years ago, a case which I easily solved of course". He then went on to tell a story about a milk deliveryman and his stolen horse, the tale bore no relation to Cormacs problem at all. "And not alone did I get his horse back I was clever enough to find the tail the next day. That, my friends, was a red-letter day in the history of criminal investigation let me tell you that I, Umbhar, is no dope". Cormac and Orla looked at each other in despair.

There was a knock on the hidden door of the fairy fort and a woman's voice to accompany it which called out "Let me in please, I am a tired and weary from travelling the roads and I seek shelter from the elements, please let me in" The little sentry standing inside was unsure as to what he should do. He knew that nobody was allowed entry without the consent of the king and his orders were strict and written on the wall in front of the sentry was a reminder, they were very short and simple and said,

NO OTHERWORLDERS.
KEEP THE DOOR AND YOUR MOUTH SHUT.
BY ORDER, KING CORMAC.

The voice called out again only this time in a voice approaching tears. "I would plead with you to help me in my hour of need". The leprechaun sentry was young and very inexperienced [he was only three hundred and forty four years old] and without seeking King Cormacs advice

he decided to give in to the pleadings of the voice outside. On opening the door of the fairy fort the young leprechaun was confronted by a pair of very ugly Otherworlders, a man and a woman, and had to hold his breath to try to overcome the obnoxious smells coming from them, but their bodily smells were quickly supplemented by another odour from a bottle which was shoved under his nose by the woman. The last thing he remembered before passing out was seeing an enormous wart on her nose, which dwarfed all the other warts on her ugly kisser. Giles and Minkin quickly made their way through the town opening the bottles as they went, pouring the contents on the ground spreading the evil magic potion, they being sure to wear masks so as not be affected by the contents of the bottles. The only noise to be heard was the sound of snoring leprechauns.

Giles laughed a deep roaring laugh and sang along; "The Suckers", "The Suckers", "There's one born every day", "Stupid amadáns, stupid amadáns" Minkin cackled in appreciation on hearing such a funny song and complimented Giles on his genius in composing such a wonderfully funny ditty, saying, "You certainly are a genius master" That comment had the affect of giving Giles a very swollen head and he started to sing the song again only this time he danced a little dance in time to his song and the spreading of the magic potion. Giles was a very vain man.

On that very same day Shamus the head worm had been out taking the morning air [as advised by his doctor] and could not help but notice the invasion of the fort by Giles and Minkin. Seamus decided that the only thing to do was go to ground for a while. He did just that by diving back down in to the long grass as fast as he could. In the cold light of day Seamus felt that there was little that he or the other worms could do anyway.

That day the leprechauns woke up and were amazed to discover that their whole community had been turned into ducks. The quacking of thousands of ducks inside the fairy fort was very loud and proved to be more annoying to the worms than the snoring, the singing, and music.

Cormac's wonderings about the character of the spirit sitting at his table talking such rubbish were quickly interrupted by the smell of an awful odour which by now had seeped into the castle and at that time he could not help but notice that his beloved Orla had turned into a duck. He tried to talk to her but all he could manage was a series of quacks across the table. Orla quacked back at him they each not having any idea as to what the other was quacking about. Unbar looked at this scene in bewilderment, he not having the foggiest notion as to what had happened or what he could do. He reached for the bottle of wine and a glass not expecting any protest from the pair of ducks sitting at the table. The street scenes outside the castle were of sheer pandemonium with thousands of mallards, screamers, stifftails, pochards, eiders, sea ducks, and others, quacking all over the place wondering how this change had occurred. They did not know it but they were suffering the wrath of the vengeful and greedy Giles De Montefiore and his crony, Minken.

Giles rubbed his hands together in glee and wondered where the gold was stashed. The affects of his magic potion would not last forever and he did not intend to leave without the hidden treasure. He felt that it was not right or proper to try to ask a duck where the crocks of gold were hidden that could be seen to be a bit humiliating for a man of his stature.

He laughed out loud and called "Minkin I am having a quacking good time, now help me search for the gold you old hag". The smelly pair started a house to house search in their attempts to find the gold with the leprechaun ducks totally immobilised, unable to stop them. After searching many houses and finding nothing they decided to change tack and headed to the castle where they easily broke down the door and entered, hoping that this could be the place where the gold was hidden.

In the meantime, the fuzzy brained Umbhar had found Cormac's stash of best wines and decided to help himself. The sudden entrance of the uninvited Giles and Minkin did not seem strange to him at all. "Would ya like a drink neighbours?" He asked. The very wily and experienced Giles was able to spot a twit from a mile away and accepted Umbhar's offer of Cormac's wine after instructing Minkin to search the castle. Giles barely sipped from his glass but made sure to keep Umbhar's glass filled to the brim. Minkin soon returned to inform Giles that her search was in vain and that there was no gold in the castle. Giles cursed Minkin and all humanity and decided to go all the way and talk to the twit in his attempts to get the gold. "So your name is Umbhar and you are from the spirit world and are here to help"

"Yeah, and I'll tell ya something for nuttin, I'm good, in fact I am very good, and I would not be surprised if I am promoted soon, I could well finish up as head honcho over all the spirits, some time in the next few centuries anyway". He then went on to bore both Giles and Minkin to tears by telling them the story about how he traced the milk delivery mans missing horse and finishing dramatically by rising from the table to shout out, "And it was me! Me! what found the lost tail the very next day". "Where was the tail?" asked Giles. "At the back end of the horse but I found it eventually". Giles shook his head to try and stay awake while Minkin yawned loudly but Umbhar was not finished and went on, "As my mother always told me, Dopey, never look a gift horse in the mouth and all that; Dopey was her pet name for me"

Giles was getting desperately bored and wondered if stealing the gold was worth it having to listen to a stupid spirit such as the imbecile at the table. Giles figured that he had had better conversations with Minkin even when she did not talk at all.

"My beautiful helper Minkin is here to assist me to help the nice leprechauns to count and polish their gold, but as you may have observed they have all turned into ducks and I now have the problem that there is a complete lack of communication because I am not proficient in the duck language, can you help me in finding the gold so as that I can help the lovely leprechauns". Umbhar scratched his head and expressed what he thought was an intelligent look.

"I'd say that it is hidden away in some secret place, that is my expert conclusion and its based on years of investigative experience"

Giles beckoned to Minkin.

"Let us be off, this idiot is of no use to us"

But Umbhar was still talking. "Also I did hear mention of a place called "The Rock" they spoke of it just before the unfortunate feather occurrence". Giles eyes lit up with interest and greed on hearing this. He had earlier spotted a large rock standing on a hill above the leprechaun

settlement and thought "Of course, that's the obvious place to hide the gold, so cunning of the little people to choose such a spot, out in the open so nobody would suspect"
"Minkin, to the hill, now"

Giles and Minkin scrambled to the door and made for the hill in haste. On their arrival Giles ordered Minkin to push the large rock to one side and after much puffing, panting, and sweating on her part she eventually succeeded in moving the rock to reveal the entrance to a hidden cave. The cave was lit by little lights, which enabled the pair to see crocks and crocks and crocks of gold lined along the walls of the cave.

"At last, at last, my dreams have come true, I can now buy all the cornflakes in the world and corner the market, getting all the cheap child labour I want or else the children of the world will starve and that thought really plucks at the strings of my heart"
"Now boss? Asked Minkin.
"Yes" shouted Giles "Yes"

Both Giles and Minkin held their hands out wide, put their heads down and snapped their fingers together, they then disappeared with all the crocks of gold, and all was left was an empty cave and a large puff of black smoke. It appeared that Giles plan to steal the gold was a complete success.

Some hours later the effects of the magic potion began to wear off and the leprechauns returned to their normal forms, bewilderment showing on their faces. Cormac and Orlas first act was to rush to the secret location deep in the hills where they had hidden the gold. All the crocks were still in their places as they expected.

The simple long-term plan to safeguard the gold had worked perfectly.

Giles and Minkin stood in Giles chamber surrounded by many crocks containing what they thought was their stolen loot. Giles could not stop laughing as they started to count the gold. On touching the first coin Giles was surprised to find that it was soft, sweet smelling, and stuck to his hand. He put it to his mouth and tasted it after which his features twisted and contorted with rage as he roared out, "Gold painted bubble gum Minkin, that's all we got, you nitwit, gold painted bubble gum, why did you not notice this trickery you hag, I do not even like bubble gum". Giles wails and cries could be heard miles away.

Things went back to normal at the fairyfort with the leprechauns soon taking up their habitual singing, music, dancing, and driving the worms crazy

The worms decided that the usual noises from the leprechauns were a lot better than the quacking of ducks and they all went to ground.

Unbhar disappeared, as did a few bottles of wine. Otherwise they all lived happily ever after {except Giles and Minkin that is}

THE END.